Dragon Slayers' Academy™ 5

KNIGHT
FOR A DAY

By Kate McMullan
Illustrated by Bill Basso

GROSSET & DUNLAP • NEW YORK

For Hilton Butchard
—K. McM.

visit us at www.abdopublishing.com

Published by Spotlight, a division of the ABDO Publishing Group, 8000 West 78th Street, Edina, Minnesota 55439. This library bound edition is published by arrangement with Penguin Young Readers Group, a member of Penguin Group (USA) Inc.

Library of Congress Cataloging-in-Publication Data
This title was previously cataloged with the following information:

McMullan, Kate.
    Knight for a day / by Kate McMullan ; illustrated by Bill Basso.
        p. cm. -- (Dragon Slayers' Academy ; 5)
    Summary: Wiglaf wins a contest that brings Sir Lancelot to the Dragon Slayers' Academy for a day, but when Wiglaf's friend Erica suspects that Lancelot is not who he claims to be trouble ensues.
        I. Basso, Bill, ill. II. Title. III. Series: McMullan, Kate. Dragon Slayers' Academy 5.
PZ7.M47879 Kn 1999
[Fic]--dc21   99-17124

ISBN 978-1-59961-377-2 (Reinforced Library Bound Edition)

All Spotlight books have reinforced library binding and are manufactured in the United States of America.

Chapter 1

"Pssst!" Wiglaf hissed at Erica. "Listen— footsteps! Mordred is coming!"

Erica paid no attention. She dipped her quill into her ink pot. She kept writing.

Wiglaf's eyes grew wide. How unlike Erica. She was a model student. She always won the Future Dragon Slayer of the Month medal.

"Hide your parchment!" warned Angus, who sat on Erica's other side. "Quickly!"

But Erica wrote on.

Wiglaf shot Angus a glance. Both boys knew how stubborn Erica could be. But they also knew that there'd be trouble if Mordred caught Erica working on another project in his How to Find Dragon Gold Class. Why, the hot-tempered headmaster might throw her into the dungeon!

Yet Wiglaf knew that if Mordred had a clue who Erica *really* was, he'd never punish her. She was Princess Erica, daughter of Queen Barb and King Ken. Girls were not allowed at Dragon Slayers' Academy, so Erica had disguised herself as a boy. Everyone there called her Eric. Wiglaf was the only DSA student who knew her secret.

The footsteps thundered closer. Then the big, bushy-haired headmaster of Dragon Slayers' Academy burst through the door.

The students jumped to attention.

All except Erica. She kept scribbling away.

"At ease, boys," Mordred said. "I bring terrible news! Twins were born last week in the village of Toenail. Twins! A bad omen, if there ever was one...er, I mean, two." Mordred looked puzzled for a moment. "In any case," he went on, "disaster has struck." His violet eyes lit upon Erica, still writing furiously. He charged across the classroom and snatched up her parchment.

"Please, sir!" Erica cried. "Let me finish!"

Mordred studied the page. Then he glared at Erica. "What is this nonsense, boy?"

"'Tis the 'Win a Knight for a Day' essay contest, sir," Erica answered. "I shall win, for the topic is 'Why I Want to Meet Sir Lancelot (The World's Most Perfect Knight).' I have hundreds of reasons!"

"Humph," said Mordred. He began reading Erica's essay aloud:

"Since my birth, I have looked up to Sir Lancelot of the Lake. The first word I spoke was 'Lancelot.' In truth I said 'Wancewot,' but I meant Lancelot. You see, like Sir Lancelot, I always tell the truth. Sir Lancelot is my shining example. No lie has ever fallen..."

As Wiglaf listened, he couldn't help but smile. Erica was crazy about Sir Lancelot. She had her Sir Lancelot Fan Club certificate nailed to the wall over her cot in the dorm. She had ordered her sword, her armor, her helmet—even her pajamas—from the Sir Lancelot Fan Club catalog.

Wiglaf had never really understood Erica's fascination with Sir Lancelot. True, Lancelot was brave. He had killed many a wicked dragon. Often he battled several rogue knights at once. And he always left them lying in pools of their own blood.

Wiglaf shuddered. The very thought of blood made him feel sick to his stomach. Clearly he was not worthy of a personal visit from the famous knight. Yet Wiglaf longed to be a hero. In fact, he had already killed two dragons. Both times had been by accident, however. So no one thought of him as a hero. He did not look like a hero, either. He was small for his age. And he had bright carrot-colored hair. But Wiglaf still had hope.

At last Mordred looked up. "What would happen if you won this contest, Eric?"

"*When* I win," Erica said, "Sir Lancelot of the Lake, the most perfect knight of all—"

"Yes, yes," said Mordred. "Get on with it."

"Sir Lancelot will come to DSA and be my knight for a day," Erica said. "He shall eat at my table. And go to class with me. And—"

"Do you think the contest winner might also get a cash prize?" the greedy headmaster cut in. "Some gold, perhaps?"

"Oh, no, sir," Erica said. "A day with Sir Lancelot is prize enough. What need would there be for gold?"

"There is always need for gold," Mordred muttered. "And yet...what fine publicity for my school if Lancelot were to come here. I could attract new students. I could raise the tuition. Yes! Lancelot must come!"

Angus groaned. "If Lancelot shows up," he whispered to Wiglaf, "Uncle Mordred will make us scrub every inch of this old castle."

Wiglaf nodded. Angus was Mordred's nephew. But this status earned him no special treatment. Quite the opposite, in fact. Angus had to help his uncle in countless ways, most of which involved scrubbing.

"I have it!" Mordred cried suddenly. "You *all* shall enter the contest! That way, one of you surely will win!"

"But *I* shall win, sir!" Erica called out.

Mordred paid no attention. "Start writing now, boys. Copy out of books if you have to. Do whatever it takes to win the prize!"

Erica rolled her eyes. But Wiglaf didn't think she looked worried. After all, who could compete with her? Erica always had a small copy of *The Sir Lancelot Handbook* with her for quick reference. She had read Sir Lancelot's memoir, *A Knight Like I*, dozens of times. Wiglaf was sure that Erica knew more about Lancelot than the knight's own mother.

Mordred turned to Erica. "When is the contest deadline?"

"All entries must be in Camelot by midnight tomorrow," Erica said.

"Bring your essays to my office first thing in the morning," Mordred told the class. "I'll have Yorick run them over to Camelot."

He rubbed his hands together. "Ha! Sir Lancelot is going to make me a rich man!"

"Sir?" called a tall, skinny boy named Torblad. "What news did you have about Toenail? I come from there, you know."

Mordred's smile faded. "The green plague has broken out in Toenail. Last time the green plague struck, boys here came down with it left and right. I had dozens of parents writing me for tuition refunds. Well, I can't have *that* happening again! So, boys, *DO NOT GET THE PLAGUE*. Do I make myself clear?"

"But, sir," said Torblad in a shaky voice. "How will we know if we have it?"

"First your tongue swells up and turns green," Mordred said.

Wiglaf tried not to think about that.

"Then," Mordred continued, "your eyes crust over with green ooze."

Wiglaf began to feel sick to his stomach.

"Your skin gets covered with green boils, and you spew whatever's in your stomach—"

That did it. Wiglaf's stomach lurched. He clapped his hand to his mouth and ran for the classroom door.

"Boy!" Mordred bellowed as Wiglaf ran by him. "Have you gone and caught the plague after I told you not to?"

Chapter 2

"Is it green?" Wiglaf stuck out his tongue.

Angus shook his head. "Trust me, Wiglaf," he said. "You don't have the green plague."

Wiglaf slumped down on his cot. He was glad he didn't have the plague. But he wished he had some excuse for running out of Mordred's class that morning. His face still burned hot with shame when he thought of it. How could he ever hope to be a hero if the mention of a few plague boils made him lose his lunch?

Wiglaf glanced down at the blank piece of parchment on his cot. He had not started his essay. And any minute, Frypot, who was on

Night Patrol for the week, would be in to put out the torches.

"There!" exclaimed Erica from her cot on the far side of the room. "Finished!" She smiled. "I've written twenty-six brilliant pages!" She hopped up and ran over to Wiglaf and Angus. She held out her essay. "Who wants to read it first?" she asked.

"Go ahead, Wiglaf," Angus offered.

"Oh, no, you first," Wiglaf said quickly.

"My conclusion is especially good." Erica sat down on Wiglaf's cot. "I don't understand why Mordred is wasting time having the rest of you write essays. Mine has winner written all over it."

Erica glanced at Wiglaf's blank parchment. "Zounds, Wiggie!" she exclaimed. "You have not written a word! Here, let me help you."

"No, I can do it." Wiglaf turned away from Erica. He dipped his quill into his ink pot. He wrote his name at the top of the parchment:

Wiglaf of Pinwick. Then he wrote: *I should like to meet Sir Lancelot, the world's most perfect knight, as I, myself, am very far from perfect.*

"You *are* very truthful," Erica said, reading over Wiglaf's shoulder. "However, in an essay, you must—"

"Nighty-night!" Frypot called from the doorway. "Into your cots, boys. Be quick about it!"

Frypot began snuffing the torches. Wiglaf put the top on his ink pot. He was glad to stop writing, for he had nothing more to say about Sir Lancelot.

The next morning, Wiglaf, Angus, and Erica hurried to the headmaster's office to turn in their essays.

Angus knocked on Mordred's door.

There was no answer.

He cracked open the door. He stuck his head in. "Uncle?" he called.

"Quiet, boy!" Mordred snapped. "Can't you see I'm counting?"

Angus opened the door wider.

Wiglaf saw that Mordred was counting tall stacks of gold coins.

"Fifty-six, sixty-eight," Mordred muttered. "Oh, jester's bells! Now I shall have to start all over!" He scooped up his gold and dumped it into a big sack. He carried the sack to his safe. "Don't look, boys!" he growled. "No one knows the combination to my safe. And I want to keep it that way."

Wiglaf turned away. He heard clicking sounds as Mordred opened his safe. A thud told him the bag of coins had landed on the safe floor. Then the heavy door slammed shut.

"Well?" Mordred glared at the students. "What is so important that you had to interrupt my morning count?"

"We have brought our essays, sir," Erica

said. "And *here* is the winner!" She proudly placed her stack of parchment on his desk.

"Ah, yes!" Mordred said. "The contest."

Other students appeared at the door. They, too, laid their essays on Mordred's desk. Then they hurried away. Wiglaf was the last to add his parchment to the stack.

Mordred stepped over to a window. He stuck out his head.

"Yorick!" he bellowed. He drew in his head. "Why is that blasted scout never around when I need him?" Mordred scratched his beard thoughtfully. "Humph. Yorick was in Toenail last week. I hope he hasn't caught the plague. It would be just like him to drop dead and not let me know."

Wiglaf hoped Mordred would not go on and on about the plague. Already he could feel his breakfast churning in his stomach.

There was a sudden knock at the door.

"Enter!" Mordred bellowed.

The door swung open. At first Wiglaf saw no one. Then, on the floor, he saw a misshapen green lump. Wiglaf gasped. The lump was human! It could be only one thing—a victim of the deadly green plague!

Wiglaf drew back. The person's skin was thick with green boils. And the poor fellow's hands had turned into flippers! Mordred had not mentioned that hideous symptom.

"You bellowed, sir?" asked the lump.

"I did, Yorick," the headmaster exclaimed.

Wiglaf went limp with relief. He realized that it was only Yorick wearing a disguise. The scout's face was smeared with green goo. And what Wiglaf had taken for infected skin was a green polka-dotted toad suit.

"These are contest entries, Yorick," Mordred said. He picked up the stack of parchment from his desk.

"Careful, sir!" Erica cautioned. "Keep my twenty-six pages together!"

Mordred handed the essays to Yorick. "Take these to Camelot," he said. "They must arrive by midnight tonight."

"Tonight?" Yorick said. "But I've got my card game tonight!"

"Yorick..." Mordred said in what Wiglaf recognized as a warning tone.

"Yes, sir." Yorick sighed. "Ribbit, ribbit." He rolled up the parchments. He stuck them into the leg of his toad suit. Then he hopped out the door.

"Don't catch the green plague on the way there, Yorick!" Mordred called after him. Then he turned to his students. "Off to class with you now, boys," he added. "Go on! Out of my sight! Shoo! Shoo! Go!"

Chapter 3

Wiglaf, Erica, and Angus hurried out of Mordred's office. They raced up the East Tower staircase to Sir Mort's class.

Sir Mort stood behind his desk. As always, the old knight wore a full suit of armor.

"Take your seats, lads," Sir Mort called. "What I mean to say is, sit down in them."

Erica always sat in the front row. But today she walked to the back of the room. She sat down in the last row. Wiglaf and Angus exchanged puzzled glances. Then they followed her, taking seats in the last row, too.

Wiglaf was about to ask Erica the meaning

of her strange behavior. But Sir Mort began banging on his helmet with his sword, which was his way of quieting the class.

"Stalking a dragon is an art, lads," the old knight said when the boys settled down. "Not everyone can do it. No, siree."

Wiglaf listened eagerly. Stalking a Fire-Breather was his favorite class. He believed that he had a talent for stalking.

"A stalker needs a good ear to hear a dragon in the brush," Sir Mort said.

Wiglaf smiled. He had excellent hearing.

"A stalker needs a good eye to follow tracks," Sir Mort added. "And, once he spots a dragon, he must stalk it without a sound."

Again Wiglaf smiled. Back home in Pinwick, he often walked very quietly so he would not be noticed by his twelve rough brothers.

"Armor clanks like a horse with bells on," Sir Mort said. "So what is the first thing a stalker must do? Take off his boots."

"P.U.!" Angus whispered to Wiglaf. "What is that awful smell?"

Wiglaf sniffed. Yuck! Had Sir Mort taken off his boots? No, that wasn't it. Wiglaf glanced at Erica. She was rubbing the canteen from her tool belt with a soft cloth. Now Wiglaf recognized the smell: silver polish!

He watched as Erica held up her shiny canteen. Satisfied, she hooked it back onto her tool belt. Next she unclipped her collapsible goblet and began polishing it.

"That stinks!" Angus whispered to Erica. "Why are you polishing your tools now?"

"I have much to do before Sir Lancelot's visit," Erica replied. "My armor must shine like a mirror. I must sharpen my sword. I must reread *A Knight Like I* so that I will have every detail of Sir Lancelot's life fresh—"

Wiglaf wanted to hear Sir Mort's stalking lesson. But he couldn't. Not with Erica going on and on about Sir Lancelot.

"Are there any questions?" Sir Mort asked. Erica's hand shot up.

"Sir Mort," she said, "have you ever met Sir Lancelot?"

Wiglaf groaned. Not Sir Lancelot again!

"Lance was my student," Sir Mort said. "It was long ago. I was teaching over at Dragon Stabbers' Prep at the time. Or was it Knights Noble?" Sir Mort scratched his helmet, thinking. "In any case, he always sat in the front row, Lance did."

"Just where *I* like to sit!" Erica beamed.

"Lance answered every question," Sir Mort added. "The other lads never got much of a chance to shine. Not with Lance around."

Erica sighed. "He sounds...perfect!"

"Sir Mort?" Wiglaf put in quickly. "Can you go on about dragon stalking now?"

"Of course I can, lad." Sir Mort nodded. "I can go on and on about anything at all."

As if to prove his point, he began going on

and on about the time he stalked a family of dragons through a poison ivy patch.

Erica polished her goblet as she listened.

Wiglaf sighed. He knew that the stalking lesson was over for the day. Once Sir Mort got going on a story, there was no stopping him.

Over the next three days, Erica stepped up her preparations for Sir Lancelot's visit. She placed her Sir Lancelot action figures in the display case in the DSA lobby. She talked all the students into washing their tunics in the moat. But when she tied feathers to the end of Wiglaf's sword and sent him forth to rid the castle of cobwebs, Wiglaf could take no more. He sneaked off to see his pet pig.

"Daisy!" he called as he entered the hen-house where she lived. "Come to me, girl!"

Daisy trotted out to greet her master.

"Iglaf-way!" she cried happily.

Wiglaf had brought Daisy with him to DSA

from Pinwick. On the way, a wizard had cast a spell on Daisy, giving her the power of speech. She now spoke perfect Pig Latin.

The two sat down together in a cozy corner of the henhouse for a long talk. Wiglaf often told Daisy things he could tell no one else.

"Erica polished her armor," Wiglaf said. "Then she polished Sir Mort's armor with him in it. The school stinks of silver polish."

Daisy wrinkled her snout. "Ee-pay oo-yay!"

"Erica is working on a welcome cheer for Sir Lancelot," Wiglaf went on. "She is forever chanting bits of it, trying to get it right." He sighed. "And every night she reads aloud from Sir Lancelot's memoir."

"Ow-hay illing-thray!" Daisy exclaimed.

"But it is *not* thrilling," Wiglaf said. "Sir Lancelot wins every battle. He slays every dragon. Every damsel falls madly in love with him. He is always so..."

"Erfect-pay," Daisy suggested.

"Yes," Wiglaf agreed. "Perfect."

Wiglaf was sick of hearing about Sir Lancelot. *And yet*, he thought, *how very fine to be a perfect knight.*

"You, carrot top." Sir Mort pointed to Wiglaf the next day in Stalking Class. "Show the class the Stealth Stalk, lad."

Wiglaf leaped to his feet. His heart thumped with joy. He quickly pulled off his boots. He stood by Sir Mort, ready to stalk.

"Here's a sly way to go after a dragon," Sir Mort told the class. "Ready?"

"Yes, sir," Wiglaf said. He bent his knees. He put his left foot in front of his right. He put his right foot in front of his left.

Suddenly a trumpet blast split the air.

Everyone ran to the window—except for Wiglaf. He stood frozen to the spot, unsure whether to keep stalking.

"What is it, lads?" Sir Mort called.

"It's a messenger," Angus said. "He is riding toward the castle gate."

"He is waving a white banner," Torblad added. "It has a red letter *C* in the middle."

"That's the flag of Camelot!" cried Erica. "The messenger is coming to tell me that I have won the Sir Lancelot contest!"

"Class dismissed!" Sir Mort said.

With that, the students ran down the tower stairs, with Erica in the lead. Angus somehow managed to keep up with her. Wiglaf brought up the rear. He felt bad that his Stealth Stalk demonstration had been interrupted.

But once outside, Wiglaf couldn't help catching the spirit of the day. Boys spilled out of every classroom into the castle yard talking excitedly. They ran toward the gatehouse.

Mordred was directing two student teachers who were cranking down the drawbridge.

Erica pushed her way between them. She grabbed the badly rusted handle and began cranking, too. That sped things up quite a bit.

"The bridge is down!" Mordred called at last. "Throw open the castle gates!"

Wiglaf heard the sound of horse's hooves on the wooden bridge. Then the messenger, his banner flying, galloped into the castle yard.

"Hear ye! Hear ye!" he called. "I bear good news for one lucky boy!"

"For me!" Erica cried. "Let's have it!"

The messenger jumped off his horse. He pulled a parchment scroll from his saddlebag. He unrolled it and began to read: "Sir Lancelot, the world's most perfect knight, shall spend the day here with the contest winner. He will arrive tomorrow."

"Tomorrow!" Erica gasped. "Zounds! I shan't sleep a wink tonight."

"That means we won't either," Angus mumbled to Wiglaf.

"The winning essay," the messenger went on, "was written by..." He stopped and looked around. Not a sound could be heard. The boys stood still as statues. The messenger glanced at his scroll. "By... Wiglaf of Pinwick!"

A stunned silence filled the castle yard.

"What?" Erica cried when she found her voice. "Is this some kind of a joke?"

That has to be it, Wiglaf thought. *A joke.*

"Knights never joke," the messenger said.

"But... but... but..." Erica sputtered. She was so undone she could hardly speak. "I saw what Wiglaf wrote. It was one sentence long!"

"That is true," Wiglaf put in. He hoped this matter would get straightened out quickly. He did not like the look on Erica's face.

"I deserve to win," Erica growled. "My essay was twenty-six pages long!"

"Well, Sir Lancelot isn't much of a reader," the messenger said. "Doesn't have the time, being a man of action and all. He likes a short

essay. And Wiglaf of Pinwick's was short. Plus it was on top of the pile. So that's the one Sir Lancelot picked."

Erica glared at Wiglaf. "This is so unfair!"

"Sir Lancelot will arrive before lunch tomorrow," the messenger went on. "Here is the schedule he likes for his visits."

The messenger handed a sheet of parchment to Wiglaf. Then he remounted his horse and galloped away.

Dazed, Wiglaf looked at the parchment:

Schedule for a Sir Lancelot School Visit

12:00 to 12:30: Welcoming Ceremony

12:30 to 2:00: Luncheon for Sir Lancelot (boarburger, potatoes fried in duck fat, garlic milk shake). After lunch, Sir Lancelot will speak for an hour.

2:00 to 4:00: Afternoon classes

4:00 to 5:00: Rest hour (students only)

5:00 to 6:00: All-school Sir Lancelot Fair Bring your pennies, lads! When you see all the fine wares for sale, you'll say, "Gadzooks!" Sir Lancelot will sell and sign copies of his best-selling memoir,

A KNIGHT LIKE I!

6:00 to 8:00: Big Feast for Sir Lancelot (boarburger with cheese, onion rings fried in goose fat, garlic milk shake)

8:00 to Way After Midnight: Wild Party! Jesters! Minstrels! Barrels of mead! Fetching damsels from neighboring castles! (no students allowed)

Mordred snatched the schedule.

"I must plan," he muttered as he read it. "And quickly!" He eyed the students, still gathered in the castle yard. "All right, boys!" he shouted. "Classes are canceled for the rest of the day! Report to the kitchen. On the double! Frypot will give out cleaning supplies. I want this castle scrubbed from top to bottom! I want DSA to shine like gold!"

Angus groaned. "What did I tell you?"

Wiglaf nodded. He had no love for scrubbing. But he was more worried about spending a day with Sir Lancelot. What would he and the great knight do? Well, he might amaze Sir Lancelot with Daisy. After all, a talking pig *is* something special. But what if Sir Lancelot wanted to joust with him? Or do some other knightly activity? Wiglaf frowned. It might be a very long day indeed.

"Move!" Mordred shouted. "Move!"

Wiglaf, Angus, and Erica began jogging toward the kitchen with the other students.

"I smell a rat!" Erica grumbled as they went. "A rat named Wiglaf!"

"Oh, come on, Eric!" Angus said. "You heard the messenger. Wiglaf's essay was on top of the pile. That's why Lancelot picked it."

"Only a goosewit would call it an essay," Erica hissed.

"I call it a big mistake," Wiglaf said quickly. "But look at the bright side. We three are best friends. So Sir Lancelot shall spend the day with all three of us."

"Humph!" Erica snorted. She seemed to want Sir Lancelot all to herself.

Frypot stood by the kitchen door, handing out cleaning supplies.

"Sir Lancelot will be staying in the Rose Chamber, North Tower," Frypot said. "You're to wash the chamber floor, Eric." He thrust a mop at her. "And Angus? Here are some brushes and lye. Mordred asked that you personally clean Lancelot's privy."

"What did I tell you?" Angus said again.

"Let me see.... Wiglaf?" Frypot squinted at his list. "Oh, you're excused from clean-up."

Excused? Wiglaf's mouth dropped open in surprise. Then he smiled. Maybe winning a knight for a day was not such a bad thing after all.

Chapter 4

"Look!" Wiglaf cried the next day as the castle bell rang noon. He pointed down Huntsman's Path. "A cloud of dust."

"I see it!" Angus said.

The dust cloud grew larger. Soon Wiglaf made out the shape of a knight on a steed. Two men rode behind him in a wagon.

"It's him," Erica breathed. "Him!"

Wiglaf's heart thumped with excitement as Sir Lancelot galloped into view. The visor on the knight's helmet was down. He wore armored gloves on his hands. No part of him could be seen. Yet inside that armor, Wiglaf knew, was Sir Lancelot of the Lake.

Sir Lancelot galloped up to the waiting group. He reigned in his steed and hopped off. He pushed up his visor. And Wiglaf found himself staring into the sky-blue eyes of the world's most perfect knight.

"Welcome!" Mordred boomed. "I am Mordred the Marvelous. I am headmaster of this fine academy for boys who dream of becoming dragon slayers, like yourself."

Mordred turned to his students. "Let's give Sir Lancelot a DSA welcome, boys!" he cried. With that, the students began to shout the cheer that Erica had made up:

Give a holler! Give a cheer!
Lancelot of the Lake is here!
He's the knight above all others.
He is perfect, kind to mothers.
He never swears or drinks or gambles.
He's polite to friars and damsels.
He slays dragons, if they're evil.
He makes us proud to be medieval!

Boys from Dragon Stabbers' Prep,
They have fight and they have pep.
Boys from Knights "R" Us have spirit,
When they cheer, you sure can hear it.
But DSA—what have we got?
We have got Sir Lancelot!

Everyone whistled and clapped.

"Thank you," Sir Lancelot said. "Let me present my men. Squire Knuckle."

A yellow-haired man behind Sir Lancelot cracked his knuckles.

"And Squire Squint." Sir Lancelot nodded toward a man with long, greasy, dark hair. He wore a patch over his left eye.

Wiglaf had never seen a squire before. But neither Knuckle nor Squint fit his idea of what a squire should look like. Squire Knuckle did not seem entirely clean. Squire Squint's hair had surely never known a comb. The two attendants reminded Wiglaf of men he had seen somewhere before. But where?

He wondered if Sir Lancelot had hired these shabby squires as some sort of good deed. *Yes*, he decided. *That must be it.*

"And now," said Sir Lancelot, "the contest winner must wish to meet me."

Mordred pushed Wiglaf forward.

"I won, sir. Wiglaf of Pinwick," Wiglaf managed. He bowed.

"Rise, Wiglaf of Pinwick!" the knight said.

Wiglaf straightened up.

"How lucky you must feel, boy," Sir Lancelot went on, "winning *me* for a day."

"Lucky is right," Erica muttered.

The knight turned to address the group. "How many of you boys have ordered items from my catalog?" he asked.

Erica's hand shot up. Sir Lancelot smiled. "Very nice," he said. "You shall get a ten-percent discount at the Sir Lancelot Fair this afternoon."

"Oh, thank you, sir!" Erica exclaimed.

"The rest of you boys will have a chance to buy Lancelot collectibles, too," he added. He turned to Knuckle. "Tell the boys what we've brought for the Sir Lancelot Fair, Squire."

"Tooooday," Squire Knuckle began, "we have a cartful of brand-new items! You can buy exact copies of Sir Lancelot's boyhood slingshot. He used it to knock out his first dragon, Snaggletooth. It comes in lead, copper, and silver. Or, for those of you with great big allowances..." Squire Knuckle grinned, "...it also comes in gold!"

"Oh!" Mordred let out a little squeal.

Again, the boys yelled and clapped.

Wiglaf clapped along with them, even though he had no allowance at all.

"And now, sir knight," said Mordred, "let us be off to lunch. I know you shall be pleased with what Chef Frypot has created for you!"

"*Chef* Frypot?" said Angus as they walked to the DSA dining hall. "Oh, puh-lease!"

"Greetings, Sir Lancelot!" said Frypot. He bowed as the great knight entered the dining hall. For once, the cook had on a clean apron.

Frypot led Sir Lancelot, the squires, Mordred, Wiglaf, Erica, and Angus to a table. They all sat down. Sir Lancelot took off his helmet. His shining black hair hung to his shoulders. He had a dimple in the middle of his perfect chin. He was very handsome.

Frypot brought Sir Lancelot's boarburger, fries, and garlic milk shake.

"I'll have the same," said Squire Knuckle, cracking his knuckles.

"Me, too," said Squire Squint. "And make sure my plate is clean."

Frypot hurried off. A minute later he came back with the squires' lunches.

"Here you go," said Frypot. "Now who gets the clean plate?"

"Chef Frypot!" Mordred exclaimed. "I'm sure all our plates are clean!"

"Uh...right," said Frypot.

The students had to line up for their usual lumpen pudding lunch. But Wiglaf didn't mind. He was so dazzled by the great knight that he could not eat a bite.

As Wiglaf sat down again, Squire Squint reached across him and grabbed the salt. Then he lunged across the table for the pickles.

"Squire Squint!" said Lancelot. "Don't reach! You have a tongue, don't you?"

"Sure," said Squint. "But my arm's longer!"

The two squires snorted with laughter.

Wiglaf's eyes grew wide. Why, these squires made *awful* jokes—just like his father and his mead-drinking buddies back in Pinwick!

After lunch, Mordred stood up. He banged his spoon on his goblet.

"Settle down, boys!" he boomed. "Unless you want double scrubbing class."

Instantly, the dining hall quieted.

"I know you are excited about our special

visitor," Mordred said. "So here, up close and personal, is the world's most perfect knight—numero uno!—to tell you what it was like growing up to be Siiiiir Lancelot!"

Everyone clapped.

Sir Lancelot stood up. "Thank you," he said. "I know how happy you must be to have me here. DSA reminds me so of Knights Noble Conservatory."

Sir Lancelot talked about his school days. How he loved spelling bees. How proud he felt when he joined the Clean Plate Club. How he always did twice as many long division problems as the teacher assigned to prove that for him, nothing was impossible.

"On holidays," Sir Lancelot said, "I loved going home to see my family. And my dog, Little Muffy. I'll stop now," he added. "For I promised to speak for an hour. And, being a perfect knight, I always keep my promises."

Erica looked puzzled. "Sir?" she said. "Wasn't your dog's name Little Scruffy?"

Sir Lancelot frowned. "Hmm, Little Scruffy. Let me think…. Ah! Little Scruffy came after Little Muffy. And before Little Puffy. He was a fat one, Little Puffy was."

"I see." Erica nodded. "Thank you, sir. I have some more questions. The first is…"

"Sorry, Eric," Mordred cut in. "But we've run out of time. Thank you, Sir Lancelot!"

Everyone clapped again. The sound rang in Wiglaf's ears. To think it was his essay that had won the contest! It was he who had brought Sir Lancelot to DSA. How proud Wiglaf felt, sitting next to the world's most perfect knight. How very far he had come from his humble birth on the cabbage farm in Pinwick.

Chapter 5

"Which classroom shall I show my handsome face in first?" Sir Lancelot asked Wiglaf as they left the dining hall.

"Weapons class, sir," Wiglaf answered. "Last week we learned sword sharpening."

"I am far too important to sharpen my own sword," Sir Lancelot said. "But it is good to know how, in case you have no squires."

They started up the East Tower stairs. Sir Lancelot's heavy boots clanked loudly as he climbed. At last they reached the classroom.

Master X, the weapons teacher, stood gazing out the window. Master X had been teaching at DSA only a short time. Before that, he had been an executioner. He was retired now, which made him an ex-executioner. But he had never lost the habit of wearing a black hood over his head.

Sir Lancelot took one look at Master X and quickly drew his sword.

"Unmask yourself, knave!" he cried. "Or I shall run you through!"

"Easy, sir knight!" said Master X, his voice slightly muffled by the hood. "Once I might have chopped off your head. Whacko!" Master X sliced an imaginary ax through the air. He chuckled. "But now I am retired."

Sir Lancelot slowly lowered his sword.

Erica and Angus had saved two seats in the front row. Wiglaf and Sir Lancelot sat down.

"Our lesson today is on daggers," said Master X. "Daggers aren't much use at an execution. All that jabbing is too messy. But if you are fighting a dragon and you drop your sword, a dagger can come in handy. Pay attention," he added, "or it's off with your heads!" Master X laughed. "Just joking! Now, who can tell me the difference between a dagger and a sword?"

"I can!" Erica called out. "A dagger has a shorter blade than a sword."

"Correct," said Master X.

"Both sides of a dagger blade are sharp," Erica added. "And the tip is pointy."

Erica is such a show-off! Wiglaf thought. He hoped that Sir Lancelot was not impressed.

"Correct, Eric." Master X nodded his hood. "Let's have a little jabbing practice."

Angus passed around a box filled with daggers. Everybody took one. Wiglaf hated to think of jabbing anything. But he took one, too.

"Who would like to demonstrate the short jab?" asked Master X.

"I might as well do it," Sir Lancelot offered. "After all," he went on, "no one else can wield a dagger as well as I." He stood up. "I hold my dagger with the handle pressed against my well-shaped wrist, like so." Sir Lancelot showed the class how he held it. "I start with my palm down. Then I lunge forward, twisting the dagger so my thumb ends up on top." Sir Lancelot jabbed at the air.

"Excuse me, sir," Erica said, once more looking puzzled. "Why do you hold the dagger in your left hand when you are right-handed?"

"Ah, why, indeed?" the perfect knight said with a small laugh. "You're a lad who pays attention, aren't you?"

Erica beamed at this praise.

Wiglaf slouched down in his seat. *Erica is getting all the attention*, he thought.

"You see," Sir Lancelot said, "when I fight lesser knights—and what knight is not lesser than I?—I hold my weapon in my left hand. It gives others a fighting chance to beat me—though no one ever has."

"Oh, you *are* kind, sir!" Erica cried.

"Yes," Sir Lancelot agreed. "That I am."

The class practiced jabbing then. Sir Lancelot helped Wiglaf with his jab.

"You've got it!" the knight said at last.

Wiglaf had never felt so proud. For once he was sorry to hear the bell ring.

"Class dismissed!" said Master X. "Drop your daggers in the box as you leave. Or I'll decapitate you!" The ex-executioner laughed darkly as the students hurried away.

"Which class shall I grace next?" Sir Lancelot asked Wiglaf.

"Stalking," Wiglaf said. "In the tower."

"So we climb, eh?" said Sir Lancelot. And once more he clanked his way up the stairs.

Wiglaf, Erica, and Angus followed.

"Sir Lancelot?" Erica said. "Do you remember Sir Mort, your old teacher?"

"Of course I do!" exclaimed Sir Lancelot.

"I shall present you to him," Erica added. "How happy he shall be to see you again."

Wiglaf frowned. He had arranged for Erica to be near Sir Lancelot for the whole day. But he was the contest winner after all. He did not want Erica to take over his knight. At a bend in the stairs, he pulled her aside.

"I am Sir Lancelot's host," he said. "Maybe I should present him to Sir Mort."

"All right," Erica snapped. "Be that way."

She climbed the rest of the way in silence.

"Come in, lads. Come in." Old Sir Mort greeted his students at the doorway. "It's a lovely day for stalking."

"Sir Mort?" Wiglaf said. "May I present your former pupil, Sir Lancelot?"

Sir Mort looked closely at the visitor.

"I remember you!" he said at last. "The lad with the awful cough. Always hocking things up from the back of your throat."

Wiglaf groaned. Oh, why had he not let Erica present Sir Lancelot to Sir Mort?

"No, no," said Sir Lancelot. "It was Lance of the Field who had the cough. I am Lance of the Lake. I was never sick. I sat in the front row and answered every question."

"*That* Lance!" Sir Mort said. "Why didn't you say so? Sit down, lads. Let's begin."

Wiglaf and Sir Lancelot found seats.

"Who would like to show me the Quick Stalk?" Sir Mort said.

Wiglaf raised his hand. If only Sir Mort would call on him! He could show Sir Lancelot that he was an excellent stalker.

"I shall," Sir Lancelot offered. "For who could do it better than I?"

"Off with your boots, then," said Sir Mort.

"Oh, but I stalk with my boots on," said Sir Lancelot.

"Not in *my* class, you don't!" cried Sir Mort. "I remember you now. You never listened.

Always a big know-it-all." He turned to Wiglaf. "You show us, lad."

Wiglaf did not want to take Sir Lancelot's place. But he did want to show off his stalking skill. He rose and kicked off his boots. He was glad he had worn his socks without holes today. He bent his knees. He began moving— left foot, right foot—silently across the room.

"Fine form, Wiglaf!" said Sir Mort.

Wiglaf thought he might burst with pride. At last, here was his moment to shine!

But what a brief moment it was.

For Erica raised her hand.

"Didn't you ask for the Quick Stalk, sir?" she said. "Wiglaf is stalking very slowly."

"Speed is important," Sir Mort agreed. "But so is keeping your ears open. That's the main thing, lads. Keep your ears open. Keep your eye to the ground. Keep your nose clean. And keep your cash in the heel of your boot.

That's where I keep mine." Sir Mort gazed out at his students. "Any questions, lads?"

After Stalking Class, Wiglaf and Sir Lancelot walked down the stairs together.

"Sir Lancelot?" Wiglaf said. "Before rest hour begins, I have something to show you."

"I hope it is something worth showing me, Wiglaf of Pinwick," said Sir Lancelot.

"Oh, it is, sir," Wiglaf said. He liked being called Wiglaf of Pinwick. It sounded far more grand than plain old Wiglaf. Maybe he would ask everyone to call him Wiglaf of Pinwick.

Yes! It was time for a change. It was time Wiglaf of Pinwick started getting a little respect around here.

Chapter 6

"We've been waiting for you, sir," said Squire Knuckle. He stood beside Squire Squint at the bottom of the tower stairs. "We've set up for your book signing at the fair."

Wiglaf stared at the squires. There was something so familiar about them!

"Wiglaf says he has something to show me," Sir Lancelot said. He turned to Wiglaf. "Perhaps my squires could come along?"

"Of course," Wiglaf said. He had hoped to be alone with the great knight. But he hid his disappointment as he led the way outside.

"What's this?" said Squire Knuckle when they reached the henhouse. "A chicken coop?"

"Yes, sir," Wiglaf said. They went inside. The hens sat on their nests clucking happily.

"Tell me, lad," said Knuckle. "Which side of a chicken has the most feathers?"

"That's hard to say, sir," Wiglaf answered.

"The outside!" cried Knuckle.

The squires laughed loudly.

Wiglaf rolled his eyes. In truth, these squires told *worse* jokes than his father.

"Daisy!" Wiglaf called. "Come, girl!"

Wiglaf heard the patter of hooves. Daisy rounded the corner—and skidded to a stop. Her eyes grew wide with fear.

Wiglaf put his arm around Daisy's neck. "Sir Lancelot," he said, "this is Daisy."

"What a fine pig," said the knight.

"Nice and fat," commented Squire Knuckle.

"Yummy!" said Squire Squint.

Daisy gave a little squeal.

"You mustn't say things like that," Wiglaf said quickly. "Daisy is no ordinary pig. She is my best friend. And she can talk." He gave Daisy a pat. "Say hello, girl."

Daisy kept her terrified eyes on Wiglaf. She kept her mouth firmly closed.

"Go on," Wiglaf urged. "Say something."

"Speak up, porky!" said Squire Squint.

"Daisy, please!" Wiglaf begged.

"Oink-yay," Daisy said at last.

Wiglaf looked over at Lancelot. The world's most perfect knight did not look impressed.

Wiglaf managed a small laugh. "Speak, Daisy. Talk to Sir Lancelot."

But Daisy scooted out from under Wiglaf's arm and ran to the back of the henhouse.

"'Bye-'bye, bacon!" Squint called after her.

"Really, she can speak," Wiglaf said.

"If you say so," the knight said. But he winked at his squires.

Wiglaf groaned. Clearly Sir Lancelot did not believe him. He felt like a fool!

Wiglaf lay on his cot at rest hour. He didn't blame Daisy for not talking. Not after the squires' rude remarks. Maybe if he brought Sir Lancelot to the henhouse by himself, Daisy would speak. That would impress Sir Lancelot. And Wiglaf very much wanted to impress the famous knight.

The end-of-rest-hour bell rang. The students jumped up from their cots.

"It is time for the Sir Lancelot Fair!" Erica cried. "Come! Let us be off!"

Wiglaf, Erica, and Angus ran down the stairs and out to the castle yard. They stopped, amazed. Long tables had been set up and draped in gay colors. Every table was piled high with official Sir Lancelot products.

"I am glad that I saved every cent Uncle Mordred has paid me for working these last three years!" Angus exclaimed. He opened his hand. In it lay three copper pennies.

"Boys! Over here!" called Squire Squint.

They hurried over to his table.

"Look," said the squire. He held up a small wooden whistle. "The official Sir Lancelot duck call. Only two pennies."

Erica looked puzzled. "I don't remember that in the catalog," she said. "When would Sir Lancelot ever want to call ducks?"

"When he has soup and wants some quackers!" cried Squire Squint. He slapped his knee, laughing. "All right," he went on. "Who wants a jar of Sir Lancelot elephant repellant?"

"But there isn't an elephant within miles of DSA!" Angus exclaimed.

"See? It works!" cried Squint. "Here, lad. Buy this pair of Sir Lancelot fuzzy dice!"

He handed Wiglaf a string that held two big furry red dice with white spots.

"Just six pennies!" the squire added.

"I have never seen fuzzy dice in the Sir Lancelot catalog, either," Erica remarked.

"They're new!" Squint said. "Tie them to

your sword for luck. Or to ward off the green plague. Who wants the dice?"

"I should like to have them," Wiglaf said. "I have no pennies, but—"

Squint quickly grabbed the dice back. He dangled them in front of Angus.

Angus looked down at his three pennies.

Squint, too, eyed the pennies.

"For you," he said, "half price."

"Oh, thank you, Squire!" Angus exclaimed.

Squint quickly pocketed Angus's pennies.

He turned to Erica. "And for you? How about a nice Sir Lancelot souvenir tunic?"

He held up a white tunic. Black letters on it spelled out: *My brother met Sir Lancelot and all I got was this lousy tunic.*

"No, thanks," Erica muttered. "Not even with my ten-percent discount." She turned to Wiglaf and Angus. "Come on, let's go."

The three walked all around the fair. They passed student teachers selling Sir Lancelot mead mugs. They saw Squire Knuckle selling bottles of Sir Lancelot Sure-Thing Wart Cure. Beside him was a stack of Sir Lancelot cart bumper stickers. They said: "I ♥ Sir Lancelot!"

Wiglaf saw Mordred showing a group of boys and their parents around the castle yard.

"Knights of the Round Table often drop in to visit us here at DSA," he told them. "They never go to Dragon Stabbers' Prep. Or Knights "R" Us."

Angus rolled his eyes. "Uncle Mordred is making the most of having Sir Lancelot here!"

"We have fairs like this all the time," Mordred went on. "My students are happy boys. They love school!" He smiled at the parents. "Now, what do you say we go into my office and sign some papers?"

"Look, there's Sir Lancelot," Angus said.

The knight sat at a table at the far end of the yard. He was surrounded by stacks of *A Knight Like I*. Dozens of DSA students were lined up to buy books and have them auto-graphed. A sign above the table read:

Book: 10 pennies
Signed book: 20 pennies

Angus whistled. "Twenty pennies! That is a sky-high price!"

"'Tis indeed," Erica agreed. "My copy cost only three pennies."

Wiglaf wished he had ten pennies so that he might buy a book. But he had never seen that much money at one time in his life.

Sir Lancelot glanced up. He beckoned. "Over here!" he called. "I need some help!"

"Let's go!" exclaimed Erica.

"I think he means me," Wiglaf said. "The contest winner."

"That again!" Erica grumbled. "Come on, Angus. It's Frypot's turn in the dunking booth. And I feel like dunking someone!"

Wiglaf trotted over to Sir Lancelot. "How can I help you, sir?"

"I shall sign my great name in each book," the knight said. "Then you shall blow on the ink to dry it."

And so, for the rest of the fair, Wiglaf huffed and puffed. He grew dizzy and weak from lack of breath. But he didn't mind. Helping Sir Lancelot was its own reward.

That night, Wiglaf walked into the dining hall with Sir Lancelot. Flames from many torches lit the room. Red-and-white Camelot shields hung on the walls. Wiglaf and the knight made their way to the head table. Boys clapped as they walked by.

So this is fame, thought Wiglaf. He liked the feel of it.

Angus and Erica stood at their places. When Sir Lancelot took his seat, everyone sat down. Frypot hurried over, carrying Sir Lancelot's boarburger with cheese and onion rings.

"Here you are, sir!" Frypot said. He set the

plate down in front of the knight. "I made a special mushroom sauce for your burger."

"Why, thank you," said Sir Lancelot. He reached for his boarburger.

But suddenly Erica drew her sword and whacked Sir Lancelot's plate across the table. His boarburger hit the floor—splat!

"Knave!" Sir Lancelot leapt up and drew his sword. "You dare to attack my supper?"

"I saved you from the mushrooms, Sir Lancelot!" Erica cried.

"Mushrooms?" Sir Lancelot said. "I am very fond of mushrooms."

"But sir!" Erica said. "You are horribly allergic to them! On page ninety-seven of *A Knight Like I*, you tell of the time you found a clump of mushrooms in the Dark Forest. Do you not remember, sir? They made you deathly ill!"

Sir Lancelot lowered his sword. "Ah," he said. "What a careful reader you are, boy."

Erica beamed. "Thank you, sir."

Wiglaf sighed. How could he ever hope to impress Sir Lancelot with Erica around?

"But that time in the forest," Sir Lancelot went on, "I ate a rare wild mushroom. That is the only kind that bothers me."

"Sit down, Eric!" Mordred boomed. "Frypot! Another boarburger with cheese for Sir Lancelot. Medium rare. And make it snappy!"

Erica slowly sat back down.

"Nice try," Angus told her.

Wiglaf felt bad for Erica. But she was so greedy for attention. If only she could give it up and accept that he was the contest winner. Then things would go much better for her.

For the rest of the meal, Erica muttered darkly to herself while she pushed her lumpen pudding around on her plate.

Wiglaf lay on his cot in the dorm. He heard laughter and goblets clinking. A minstrel's songs floated up from the castle yard.

"It sounds like a fine party," said Angus.

"It does," Wiglaf agreed. But inside he felt disappointed. For surely the contest winner should have been invited to the party!

Wiglaf glanced over at Erica. She had been sitting on her cot thumbing through *A Knight Like I* for hours. Suddenly she slammed the book shut. She hopped up and ran over to Wiglaf and Angus.

"I have grave news," she whispered.

"What?" asked Wiglaf and Angus together.

"Lancelot never had a dog named Little Muffy," Erica declared.

"That is your news?" Wiglaf groaned.

"He never had a dog named Little Puffy, either," Erica went on. "His only dog was Little Scruffy."

"What does it matter?" Angus asked. "It was long ago. Perhaps he has forgotten."

Erica shook her head. "He has a perfect

memory. And there is more. An evil knight stabbed Sir Lancelot through his left palm."

"Clearly the wound has healed," said Angus. "For we saw him wield a dagger left-handed."

"That is my point," Erica said. "It was a terrible wound. Sir Lancelot cannot hold even a spoon in his left hand. And," she continued, "all mushrooms are poison to Sir Lancelot."

"What are you saying?" asked Angus.

"I am saying," said Erica, "that this man who says he is Sir Lancelot is a fraud!"

Chapter 7

"What?" cried Wiglaf. "That is a lie!"

Erica drew herself up tall. "I have devoted my life to studying Sir Lancelot," she said. "You know nothing about him."

"I am the contest winner," Wiglaf pointed out. "You are jealous because my essay won!"

"Dream on!" Erica cried.

"Simmer down," Angus advised. "You don't want Frypot coming in to take down our names for talking."

Wiglaf and Erica glared at each other.

"That man is a fraud," Erica said at last. "And I have a way to prove it."

She opened *A Knight Like I*. She showed Wiglaf and Angus a drawing of Sir Lancelot.

Erica pointed to the knight's left heel. "If this man has a sword-shaped birthmark here, I will believe he is Sir Lancelot," she said. "But if he does not, it will prove he is a fake."

"How do we see his left heel?" asked Angus.

"We shall look at it while he is sleeping," Erica explained.

"What?" cried Wiglaf. "Do you mean—"

"Yes," said Erica. "We shall sneak into the Rose Chamber tonight, after the party. Sir Lancelot sleeps like a baby. Remember?"

Wiglaf groaned. What if they were caught? If only Erica were not so jealous of him. Was it his fault that he had written a brilliant essay? But if going along was the only way to convince Erica she was wrong, he guessed he'd have to do it. "All right," he said with a sigh.

The party went on and on. Wiglaf, Erica, and Angus played games to keep themselves

awake. They had no cards. And Angus refused to let them roll his fuzzy dice. So they played "Rock, Parchment, Scissors."

At last the sounds of the party faded. Soon all was still.

"All right," Erica whispered after it had been quiet for a long time. "Let's go."

The three tiptoed out into the dark hallway. Erica lit the minitorch from her tool belt. They made their way to the tower staircase. Wiglaf kept a lookout for Frypot.

They climbed the stairs to the Rose Chamber. Erica lifted the latch and pushed open the door. The three crept inside. Angus shut the door behind them.

By the light of the minitorch, Wiglaf saw Sir Lancelot. He lay face down across the big bed. He still had his armor on. But—thank goodness!—he had kicked off his boots.

The three crept noiselessly toward the bed.

Wiglaf couldn't wait to prove to Erica that this knight was indeed Sir Lancelot of the Lake.

A wheezing noise made Wiglaf freeze. Then he realized it was only Sir Lancelot snoring.

"The *real* Sir Lancelot never snores," Erica muttered. "Pull off his sock, Wiglaf."

"You do it," Wiglaf said. "This was your idea."

"Shhh!" Angus said. "I'll do it."

Angus hooked his fingers under Sir Lancelot's sock. He slowly peeled it off.

"Oh, P.U.!" Angus said, dropping the sock. "How his foot doth stinketh!"

"That's more proof!" Erica whispered. "The real Sir Lancelot's feet smell sweet."

Wiglaf drew back. In truth, Sir Lancelot's foot was anything but sweet. He bent to examine the knight's heel. And he saw...nothing.

Wiglaf stood up. Could Erica be right? Was this man a fake?

"Oops!" said Angus. "Wrong foot." He began peeling off the other sock.

Wiglaf smiled as the sword-shaped birthmark came into view.

Erica bent down to inspect the mark.

"Now will you stop saying that he is an imposter?" Wiglaf asked.

Sir Lancelot snorted and rolled over.

"Let's get out of here," Angus said.

But as they turned to go, Wiglaf heard a high-pitched noise coming from the hallway.

"How odd," he whispered. "Sounds like a pig squealing."

Suddenly there came a cracking sound. Then a loud pounding on the door.

"Get up!" called a gruff voice. "We got the gold. We must be off!"

There was that cracking noise again. Now Wiglaf knew the sound: cracking knuckles!

"Quick!" cried Angus. "Into the wardrobe!"

Erica blew out the minitorch. The three dove into the big wooden closet that stood at the foot of Sir Lancelot's bed.

And just in time, too. No sooner had they pulled the doors shut than they heard heavy footsteps inside the chamber.

Wiglaf peeked through a crack between the doors. He saw the squires. Each one had a big sack slung over his back. Wiglaf gasped. Inside one of the sacks, something was wiggling and squirming—and squealing!

It's Daisy! thought Wiglaf. *They've got Daisy!*

He burst out of the wardrobe.

"Stop! Thieves!" he cried. "Put down my pig!"

Erica rushed out behind him.

"Stop, in the name of Queen Barb and King Ken!" she called to the squires.

"Right!" said Angus, still cowering inside the wardrobe.

Knuckle drew his sword. "Get back into that closet, runts!" he yelled at them.

Squint tugged at the sleeping knight. He pulled him to his feet.

"Take the gold," Wiglaf cried. "But, please! Leave me my pig!"

"Not a chance," said Knuckle. "Into that closet, both of you!"

Knuckle lunged forward. He shoved Wiglaf and Erica back into the closet. He slammed the door. Wiglaf heard the click of the key in the lock. He pushed hard against the doors. They were locked in!

"Let's go!" said Squire Squint.

"Unhand me, man!" cried Lancelot. "Let me get my boots on!"

"There's no time!" Squint growled. "Move!"

Wiglaf's eyes grew wide. Knuckle and Squint were kidnapping Sir Lancelot!

"Farewell, runts!" Knuckle cried. "By the time you get out of there, we'll be feasting on nice juicy pork chops!"

"Nooo!" Wiglaf wailed. "Do not eat my pig!"

The door to the Rose Chamber slammed.

In a fury, Wiglaf kicked at the wardrobe

door. His foot split through a rotten board. He kept kicking. Soon he had made a sizable hole. He scrambled out through it. Erica came next, followed by Angus.

"Come on," said Erica. "We must get our swords. Then we shall capture the thieves!"

"And save Sir Lancelot!" cried Angus.

"And Daisy!" cried Wiglaf. "Poor Daisy!"

The three ran down the staircase. Wiglaf's head was spinning. He had to get to Daisy—before it was too late!

They raced out of the castle. A full moon lit their way as they ran across the castle yard.

"Look, there they are!" Wiglaf whispered. He pointed toward the gatehouse.

Lancelot stood just outside the gatehouse. He held his steed and the wagon horses. Squint and Knuckle were inside the gatehouse, bent over the drawbridge crank.

"That crank is rusted stiff," Erica said.

Wiglaf, Erica, and Angus kept to the shadows as they ran closer. They flattened themselves against the castle wall.

"We must rush them at once!" Erica said.

"Hold on," cautioned Angus. "The squires are armed and dangerous. And we are not," he pointed out. "We cannot win if we rush them."

"You may be right," said Erica. "But we must do something! They are about to escape!"

"Let us sneak up on them with the Quick Stalk," Wiglaf suggested. "That way we shall have surprise on our side."

Erica and Angus nodded.

With Wiglaf in the lead, they bent their knees and began stalking. No stalkers ever stalked more stealthily than did those three that night. Soon they could hear the thieves' voices.

"Crank it down!" Squint growled. "Hurry!"

"I'm doing my best!" Knuckle said. "I could use some help, you know."

"I can't put down this bloody pig!" Squint said. "She'll kick her way out of the bag."

Wiglaf heard Daisy squealing as they crept nearer still.

"Here it goes!" Knuckle cried suddenly.

Wiglaf heard the groan of a chain. The crank was working! He stood helplessly by as the drawbridge came down with a bang.

Wiglaf's heart pounded. He couldn't let them get away! Not with Daisy in their clutches. He had to act! He started running at the thieves. He let out a warrior's cry.

"ARRRRRRRRR!" Wiglaf roared as he ran.

Erica and Angus were right behind him. The thieves whirled around, startled.

The horses whinnied. They bolted away from Sir Lancelot, galloping for the stable.

"Come on!" cried Squint. "Let's move!"

Squint, Knuckle, and Lancelot took off running across the drawbridge.

The thieves were big and strong. But Wiglaf, Erica, and Angus were young and fast. They caught up with the thieves in the middle of the bridge. Wiglaf lunged for Daisy. He grabbed his pig and hung on for dear life.

"Gimme that!" cried Squint. He tried to pull the pig away.

But Wiglaf held on tight. He wrenched Daisy away from the thief.

Squint lost his grip on the bag, and he lost his balance. He teetered at the edge of the bridge. He windmilled his arms. But it was no use. Squint toppled off the bridge and into the moat—*splash!*

Angus grinned when he saw what had happened. Then he lowered his head and ran full speed at Knuckle. He butted him—hard!

"Ooof!" Knuckle gasped as Angus knocked the wind out of him. He let go of the gold. And he, too, fell into the moat.

"Your turn!" Erica yelled at Lancelot.

"Not I!" Sir Lancelot turned and started running back to the castle.

Erica stuck out her foot.

"Whoa!" Lancelot cried as he tripped over it. He, too, splashed into the moat. His armor made him sink up to his chin.

Wiglaf was still struggling with the knot on Daisy's sack. He heard someone running behind him. He glanced over his shoulder. He gasped. A black-hooded figure in a nightshirt was speeding toward him, swinging an ax!

"I heard a commotion, boys!" cried the axman, who, of course, was Master X. "What is it? What's going on?"

"Thieves are in the moat!" Erica cried. "Quick! They're trying to get away!"

The ex-executioner ran to the foot of the drawbridge. Erica and Angus were right behind him. They jumped off the bridge and ran to where the soaking wet thieves were crawling out of the moat.

"Not another step, scoundrels!" Master X cried from beneath his hood. "Drop your weapons! Or I shall cut off your heads and use them for bowling balls!"

Knuckle, Squint, and Lancelot quickly threw their swords onto the bank of the moat.

On the drawbridge, Wiglaf finally untied the knot that held Daisy in the bag. His pig bounded out.

"Iglaf-way!" she cried happily. "Oo-yay aved-say y-may ife-lay!"

"Daisy!" Wiglaf wrapped his arms around her. He glanced down at Sir Lancelot. "See, sir?" he said. "I told you she could talk."

Chapter 8

iglaf and Daisy jumped down from the drawbridge. They hurried over to the others.

Wiglaf stared at Sir Lancelot as he stood dripping beside the moat. He looked different somehow. He was barefoot, for one thing. And then Wiglaf realized that without his boots on, the knight was very short.

"What a good thing Frypot asked me to take night patrol for him tonight," Master X said. He took a step toward Knuckle. "I think I'll behead you first."

"Not me!" cried Knuckle. "Do Squint first!"

"Tell me who you are!" Master X demanded.

"I'm Knuckle Squeegee," Knuckle said,

cracking his you-know-whats. "And that's my baby brother, Squint."

"Squeegee!" cried Master X. "Why, I've chopped off dozens of Squeegee heads! You come from a family of robbers, cutthroats, thugs, thieves, and homicidal maniacs!"

"That's us," said Squint proudly. He yanked off his eye patch.

"Wait! I know you," Wiglaf exclaimed.

"Iglaf-way!" cried Daisy. "Int-squay and-yay Uckle-knay un-ray e-thay utcher-bay op-shay in-yay Inwick-pay!"

"The butchers of Pinwick?" Wiglaf said. No wonder Daisy had been so scared! And no wonder Knuckle and Squint looked so familiar. They *were* his father's mead-drinking buddies!

"False knight," said Erica. "Who are you?"

"I am no false knight!" Sir Lancelot said.

"The Squeegee brothers kidnapped him," Wiglaf said. "Isn't that so, sir?"

"That's it exactly," the knight agreed quickly.

"Not so!"said Erica. "Give your name!"

"He is Sir Lancelot!" Wiglaf cried. "We saw his sword-shaped birthmark."

"Birthmark smirthmark!" Erica took a step closer. "Let's have a look at it now."

"I am who I say I am," Sir Lancelot said.

"Then show us your left heel," Erica said.

"Back off, knave!" Sir Lancelot cried.

"Do as he says!" Master X demanded.

Sir Lancelot scowled. But he turned around. He held up his left foot. Wiglaf saw that the "birthmark" was half gone.

"Ake-fay ight-knay!" cried Daisy.

"A dragon spit fire at my heel," the knight said. "He burned off half my birthmark."

"The truth, sir!" Master X said, raising his ax.

"He is Leon of the Lake," Knuckle offered. "Lancelot's twin brother."

"Do not listen to him!" the knight cried.

"Lancelot is perfect," Squint added. "But Leon is perfectly awful."

Erica gasped. "You mean..."

"Yes," said Squint. "Leon is Lance's evil twin!"

Erica turned to Leon. "But Sir Lancelot makes no mention of you in *A Knight Like I*."

"Don't rub it in," Leon said sulkily. "We are twins, yet we have some differences. Lance is right-handed. I am left-handed. Lance is—"

"Tall," Erica cut in. "And you are short."

"Let Leon tell his story," Wiglaf put in quickly. After all, what was so wrong with being short?

"When we were born," Leon began, "except for the sword-shaped birthmark on Lance's heel, we looked as alike as two peas in a pod. But our father believed that twins were bad luck. So he gave me away to a peasant family passing through Camelot. He never guessed that they were Squeegees."

"Icked-way utchers-bay!" muttered Daisy.

"I had an excellent education," Leon went on. "I started out picking pockets. Moved on to snatching purses. Robbing the collection plate at church. I dabbled in highway robbery. Some hit-man jobs. The usual. But every night I came home and read *The Medieval Times*. There were always stories about Lance. Lance killing dragons. Lance saving damsels. Lance fighting ten evil knights at once."

Wiglaf felt half sorry for Leon.

"Lance became a knight," Leon went on. "Damsels fainted for love of him. Oh, how I wanted to *be* him! I wanted to know how it felt to be perfect. And then Knuckle here came up with a plan."

Knuckle cracked his knuckles. "The 'Win a Knight for a Day' contest was my idea."

Wiglaf's heart sank. Some contest winner he was. The whole thing was a scam.

"To pass for Lancelot, all I had to do was to act really, really conceited," Leon said. "And wear elevator boots."

"I should have known fuzzy dice weren't Sir Lancelot's style," Angus said glumly.

"You have on Sir Lancelot's armor, Leon," Erica pointed out. "I know it by the bud vase on the chest plate, just above the heart."

"Humph." Leon fingered the small, silver vial. "I thought it was a snuff pouch."

"It is meant to hold violets that damsels give to Sir Lancelot," Erica said. "How is it that you have on his armor?"

Leon only smirked.

Master X brandished the ax again.

"I...I hired the witch, Morgana le Fay, to put a curse on Lancelot," Leon confessed.

"A curse most foul!" cried Knuckle.

"Lance is too feather-brained to rescue damsels now!" Squint added. He and his brother cackled wickedly.

"I've heard enough!" cried Master X. "I shall execute all three of you at once!"

"But you said you were retired," Leon whined.

"I'll come out of retirement," said Master X.

"Which," he added, "will make me an ex-ex-executioner." He eyed the three thieves. "Have you robbed other schools?" he asked.

"Nah," said Squint. "This was our first. We heard that the headmaster here had lots of gold. And that he was none too clever."

"My Uncle Mordred is *very* clever," Angus said loyally.

"Where *is* Mordred anyway?" asked Erica.

"Oh, he's safe," Squint said with a wink.

"Very safe!" cried Knuckle.

The brothers laughed and slapped hands.

Daisy nudged Wiglaf. "Ordred-may is-yay in-yay is-hay afe-say!"

Wiglaf gasped. "Master X!" he cried. "They've locked Mordred in his safe!"

"We must get him out!" cried Angus.

"Don't execute anyone until we get back, Master X," Erica said. "Promise?"

"Oh, all right," said Master X grudgingly.

"I'll take these goosewits to the dungeon." The ex-executioner poked Leon with his ax. "Get a move on," he said. "Chop, chop!"

Wiglaf, Daisy, Erica, and Angus ran back toward the castle. Angus picked up Mordred's sack of gold on the way.

They burst into the headmaster's office.

"Uncle Mordred!" Angus cried.

A dull thump came from inside the safe.

"I'll get you out, Uncle!" shouted Angus.

"But how can you?" asked Wiglaf. "No one knows the combination to Mordred's safe."

"That's what he thinks," Angus said. He ran to the safe and began spinning the dial. Half a minute later—*click!*—he opened the door.

There lay Mordred on the floor of the safe. Knuckle and Squint had tied him up like a turkey. They stuffed his socks in his mouth.

"Uggggg!" Mordred said.

Daisy lay down in a corner while the three

rushed into the safe and untied Mordred. Angus yanked the socks out of his mouth.

"You peeked!" Mordred cried. He struggled to his feet. "You peeked at the combination to my safe!"

"No, Uncle!" Angus said.

"How else could you have opened the door?" Mordred bellowed. "It's the thumb screws for you, nephew!"

"No, please!" Angus begged. "You doze sometimes at your desk. You talk in your sleep. I couldn't help but hear the combination."

"A likely story," Mordred grumbled. "And what is that *pig* doing in my office?"

"Ust-jay esting-ray," said Daisy.

Suddenly Mordred's face fell. "Oh, jester's bells!" he wailed. "I'd forgotten. My gold was stolen! Every lovely coin of it is gone!"

"No, it isn't, sir," said Erica. "We caught the thieves before they left the castle." She pointed to the sack leaning against Mordred's desk. "Here is your gold."

"Oh, joy!" cried Mordred as he sprang over to it. He wrapped his arms tightly around his hoard. "My golden coins," he crooned, patting the sack gently. "Daddy's here. No one's going to take you again."

"Um, sir?" said Erica after Mordred had spent a few tender moments with his gold. "That knight is not Sir Lancelot. It's his evil twin, Leon. And Knuckle and Squint are not squires."

"You know," said Mordred, "I was beginning to suspect that."

"The real Sir Lancelot is under a terrible curse," Wiglaf added.

Erica fell to her knees. "I beg of you, sir! Send us on a quest to rescue Sir Lancelot! We must save the world's most perfect knight!"

"Hmmmm." Mordred sifted through his coins thoughtfully. "If you boys rescued him, it would look very good for the school."

"That is true, sir!" said Wiglaf.

"And surely Sir Lancelot would pay a big reward," Mordred went on.

"No doubt," said Angus.

"Well, what are you waiting for?" Mordred boomed. "Get packing! Don't loaf about here in my office. Go on your quest. Shoo!"

They all hurried out of his office.

"If you catch the green plague, don't come back!" Mordred called after them. "And don't take an I.O.U. for the reward. Make Lancelot give it to you in cash, boys! Solid gold!"

A quest! thought Wiglaf as they ran to the dorm to pack. Surely this would be the most exciting thing that had ever happened to him. Heroes went on quests. So perhaps he, Wiglaf of Pinwick, might finally become a hero.

~DSA~
YEARBOOK

Goldius est goodius!

The Campus of Dragon Slayers' Academy

DSA

Lady Lobelia's Chamber

Dr. Pluck's Science Lab

Mordred's Classroom

Tunnel Exit

Headmaster's Office

Dining Hall

To Dungeon

Stable

Castle Yard

Scrubbing Class

Practice Dragon

Yorick's Quick Change-O-Rama Camp site

$\sim$ Our Founders $\sim$

Sir Herbert Dungeonstone

Sir Ichabod Popquiz

∼ Our Philosophy ∼

Sir Herbert and Sir Ichabod founded Dragon Slayers' Academy on a simple principle still held dear today: Any lad—no matter how weak, yellow-bellied, lazy, pigeon-toed, smelly, or unwilling—can be transformed into a fearless dragon slayer who goes for the gold. After four years at DSA, lads will finally be of some worth to their parents, as well as a source of great wealth to this distinguished academy.* ** ***

* Please note that Dragon Slayers' Academy is a strictly-for-profit institution.

** Dragon Slayers' Academy reserves the right to keep some of the gold and treasure that any student recovers from a dragon's lair.

*** The exact amount of treasure given to a student's family is determined solely by our esteemed headmaster, Mordred. The amount shall be no less than 1/500th of the treasure and no greater than 1/499th.

Mordred de Marvelous

Mordred graduated from Dragon Bludgeon High, second in his class. The other student, Lionel Flyzwattar, went on to become headmaster of Dragon Stabbers' Prep. Mordred spent years as part-time, semi-substitute student teacher at Dragon Whackers' Alternative School, all the while pursuing his passion for mud wrestling. Inspired by how filthy rich Flyzwattar had become by running a school, Mordred founded Dragon Slayers' Academy in CMLXXIV, and has served as headmaster ever since.

Known to the Boys as: Mordred de Miser
Dream: Piles and piles of dragon gold
Reality: Yet to see a single gold coin
Best-Kept Secret: Mud wrestled under the name Macho-Man Mordie
Plans for the Future: Will retire to the Bahamas . . . as soon as he gets his hands on a hoard

Lady Lobelia

Lobelia de Marvelous is Mordred's sister and a graduate of the exclusive If-You-Can-Read-This-You-Can-Design-Clothes Fashion School. Lobelia has offered fashion advice to the likes of King Felix the Husky and Eric the Terrible Dresser. In CMLXXIX, Lobelia married the oldest living knight, Sir Jeffrey Scabpicker III. That's when she gained the title of Lady Lobelia, but—alas!—only a very small fortune, which she wiped out in a single wild shopping spree. Lady Lobelia has graced Dragon Slayers' Academy with many visits, and can be heard around campus saying, "Just because I live in the Middle Ages doesn't mean I have to look middle-aged."

Known to the Boys as: Lady Lo Lo
Dream: Frightfully fashionable
Reality: Frightful
Best-Kept Secret: Shops at Dark-Age Discount Dress Dungeon
Plans for the Future: New uniforms for the boys with mesh tights and lace tunics

~ Our Faculty ~

Sir Mort du Mort

Sir Mort is our well-loved professor of Dragon Slaying for Beginners as well as Intermediate and Advanced Dragon Slaying. Sir Mort says that, in his youth, he was known as the Scourge of Dragons. (We're not sure what it means, but it sounds scary.) His last encounter was with the most dangerous dragon of them all: Knight-shredder. Early in the battle, Sir Mort took a nasty blow to his helmet and has never been the same since.

Known to the Boys as: The Old Geezer
Dream: Outstanding Dragon Slayer
Reality: Just plain out of it
Best-Kept Secret: He can't remember
Plans for the Future: Taking a little nap

Coach Wendell Plungett

Coach Plungett spent many years questing in the Dark Forest before joining the Athletic Department at DSA. When at last he strode out of the forest, leaving his dragon-slaying days behind him, Coach Plungett was the most muscle-bulging, physically fit, manliest man to be found anywhere north of Nowhere Swamp. "I am what you call a hunk," the coach admits. At DSA, Plungett wears a number of hats—or, helmets. Besides PE Teacher, he is Slaying Coach, Square-Dance Director, Pep-Squad Sponsor, and Privy Inspector. He hopes to meet a damsel—she needn't be in distress— with whom he can share his love of heavy metal music and long dinners by candlelight.

Known to the Boys as: Coach
Dream: Tough as nails
Reality: Sleeps with a stuffed dragon named Foofoo
Best-Kept Secret: Just pull his hair
Plans for the Future: Finding his lost lady love

Brother Dave

Brother Dave is the DSA librarian. He belongs to the Little Brothers of the Peanut Brittle, an order known for doing impossibly good deeds and cooking up endless batches of sweet peanut candy. How exactly did Brother Dave wind up at Dragon Slayers' Academy? After a batch of his extra-crunchy peanut brittle left three children from Toenail toothless, Brother Dave vowed to do a truly impossible good deed. Thus did he offer to be librarian at a school world-famous for considering reading and writing a complete and utter waste of time. Brother Dave hopes to change all that.

Known to the Boys as: Bro Dave
Dream: Boys reading in the libary
Reality: Boys sleeping in the library
Best-Kept Secret: Uses Cliff's Notes
Plans for the Future: Copying out all the lyrics to "Found a Peanut" for the boys

~ Faculty ~

Professor Prissius Pluck

Professor Pluck graduated from Peter Piper Picked a Peck of Pickled Peppers Prep, and went on to become a professor of Science at Dragon Slayers' Academy. His specialty is the Multiple Choice Pop Test. The boys who take Dragon Science, Professor Pluck's popular class,

- **a)** are amazed at the great quantities of saliva Professor P. can project
- **b)** try never to sit in the front row
- **c)** beg Headmaster Mordred to transfer them to another class
- **d)** all of the above

Known to the Boys as: Old Spit Face
Dream: Proper pronunciation of *p*'s
Reality: Let us spray
Best-Kept Secret: Has never seen a pippi-hippo-pappa-peepus up close
Plans for the Future: Is working on a cure for chapped lips

Frypot

How Frypot came to be the cook at DSA is something of a mystery. Rumors abound. Some say that when Mordred bought the broken-down castle for his school, Frypot was already in the kitchen and he simply stayed on. Others say that Lady Lobelia hired Frypot because he was so speedy at washing dishes. Still others say Frypot knows many a dark secret that keeps him from losing his job. But no one ever, *ever* says that Frypot was hired because of his excellent cooking skills.

Known to the Boys as: Who needs a nickname with a real name like Frypot?
Dream: Cleaner kitchen
Reality: Kitchen cleaner
Best-Kept Secret: Takes long bubble baths in the moat
Plans for the Future: Has signed up for a beginning cooking class

~ Staff ~

Yorick

Yorick is Chief Scout at DSA. His knack for masquerading as almost anything comes from his years with the Merry Minstrels and Dancing Damsels Players, where he won an award for his role as the Glass Slipper in "Cinderella". However, when he was passed over for the part of Mama Bear in "Goldilocks", Yorick decided to seek a new way of life. He snuck off in the night and, by dawn, still dressed in the bear suit, found himself walking up Huntsmans Path. Mordred spied him from a castle window, recognized his talent for disguise, and hired him as Chief Scout on the spot.

Known to the Boys as: Who's that?
Dream: Master of Disguise
Reality: Mordred's Errand Boy
Best-Kept Secret: Likes dressing up as King Ken
Plans for the Future: To lose the bunny suit

Wiglaf of Pinwick

Wiglaf, our newest lad, hails from a hovel outside the village of Pinwick, which makes Toenail look like a thriving metropolis. Being one of thirteen children, Wiglaf had a taste of dorm life before coming to DSA and he fit right in. He started the year off with a bang when he took a stab at Coach Plungett's brown pageboy wig. Way to go, Wiggie! We hope to see more of this lad's wacky humor in the years to come.

Dream: Bold Dragon-Slaying Hero
Reality: Still hangs on to a "security" rag
Extracurricular Activities: Animal-Lovers Club, President; No More Eel for Lunch Club, President; Frypot's Scrub Team, Brush Wielder; Pig Appreciation Club, Founder
Favorite Subject: Library
Oft-Heard Saying: *"Ello-hay, Aisy-day!"*
Plans for the Future: To go for the gold!

Angus du Pangus

The nephew of Mordred and Lady Lobelia, Angus walks the line between saying, "I'm just one of the lads" and "I'm going to tell my uncle!" Will this Class I lad ever become a mighty dragon slayer? Or will he take over the kitchen from Frypot some day? We of the DSA Yearbook staff are betting on choice #2. And hey, Angus? The sooner the better!

Dream: A wider menu selection at DSA
Reality: Eel, Eel, Eel!
Extracurricular Activities: DSA Cooking Club, President; Smilin' Hal's Off-Campus Eatery, Sales Representative
Favorite Subject: Lunch
Oft-Heard Saying: *"I'm still hungry"*
Plans for the Future: To write *101 Ways to Cook a Dragon*

Eric von Royale

Eric hails from Someplace Far Away (at least that's what he wrote on his Application Form). There's an air of mystery about this Class I lad, who says he is "totally typical and absolutely average." If that is so, how did he come to own the rich tapestry that hangs over his cot? And are his parents really close personal friends of Sir Lancelot? Did Frypot the cook bribe him to start the Clean Plate Club? And doesn't Eric's arm ever get tired from raising his hand in class so often?

Dream: Valiant Dragon Slayer
Reality: Teacher's Pet
Extracurricular Activities: Sir Lancelot Fan Club; Armor Polishing Club; Future Dragon Slayer of the Month Club; DSA Pep Squad, Founder and Cheer Composer
Favorite Subject: All of Them!!!!!
Oft-Heard Saying: *"When I am a mighty Dragon Slayer . . ."*
Plans for the Future: To take over DSA

~ Students ~

Baldrick de Bold

This is a banner year for Baldrick. He is celebrating his tenth year as a Class I lad at DSA. Way to go, Baldrick! If any of you new students want to know the ropes, Baldrick is the one to see. He can tell when you should definitely *not* eat the cafeteria's eel, where the choice seats are in Professor Pluck's class, and what to tell the headmaster if you are late to class. Just don't ask him the answer to any test questions.

Dream: To run the world
Reality: A runny nose
Extracurricular Activities: Practice Dragon Maintenance Squad; Least Improved Slayer-in-Training Award
Favorite Subject: *"Could you repeat the question?"*
Oft Heard Saying: *"A dragon ate my homework."*
Plans for the Future: To transfer to Dragon Stabbers' Prep